An Unexpected *Love* For Christmas

Sequel to A Leap of Faith

by

Tam Yvonne

Preface

My Dear Readers, we meet again. After the success of my debut novelette, *"A Leap of Faith,"* it was not in my plans to write a sequel to the book. However, that changed rather quickly, after I started getting feedback from you all, the readers, about how much you loved the characters in the book and wanted to read more about them. Especially, "Allison." There was something about that chica that caught a lot of your attention, and the fan mail flooded my email box asking for more on her.

So, the people spoke; and I, the writer, took to pen and paper and expounded more on who Miss Allison Gallant really was and how she became the woman you all fell in love with.

I'm going to be very forthright with you all; I did not expect *"A Leap of Faith"* to be so well received. And for it to become a best-selling book was beyond my wildest dreams. Don't get me wrong, I knew it was a good story; and that it would touch someone's life, but GEESH, I had no clue of the impact the book would have on so many of you.

I am so very grateful to all of you who purchased and reviewed my book on Amazon, Barnes & Noble, Wal-Mart, etc. The feedback and just the genuine support that I have been receiving as an author/writer is very gratifying. It absolutely means the world to me, and your kindness is certainly not going unnoticed.

With that being said, as requested, you are now holding your very own copy of my novella, *"An Unexpected Love for Christmas."* The sequel to my debut book, *"A Leap of Faith."*

I pray that you love Allison even more than you did when you were first introduced to her as Leilani Hamilton's best friend and Spelman sister in *"A Leap of Faith."*

Acknowledgments

Nothing that I do in my life is done without my seeking the guidance, protection, and love of my Savior, Jesus Christ. Without the LORD as the head of my life, I am nothing; and I will FOREVER be a lover and follower of Jesus!

My precious kids, Sharon and Ellis, truly the BEST gifts I ever received, and my Shih Tzu fur baby, "Blue," who keeps the laughter going in our home. Thank you guys for supporting "Mommy" and loving me as much as I love you all.

My "sweetie-babe," Rico. Your love, understanding, encouragement, and support has been such a blessing to me. I never thought in a million years that I'd find a man with your characteristics, and I was right. I didn't find you; GOD led our paths to cross, and HE put us together, and I am so grateful to have you in my corner. My mama, Christine, for all her words of wisdom, sacrifices, and teachings. It is all appreciated and know that I did listen. Thank you for raising me *"the right way."*

My sister, La'Toya. Words cannot describe our bond. You have been there for me more times than I can count, and I will forever be grateful for our sisterly bond. My nephews, PJ & Bryson, "Tee Tee," loves you boys, very much. My fur niece and nephew "Princess" & "Beau." My brothers, sister-in-love, brother-in-love, uncles, cousins, stepfather, and extended family. When you come from a huge family, you cannot name everyone, but my Tate & Curtis families in Alabama, you all know who you are, and I love each of you so very much.

My church family, Bishop Frances V. Mills and the wonderful Tabernacle of Faith Christian Church family, and my close friends who have been in my life for several years, you know who you are.

I can now say that I have FANS of my writing, and I want to acknowledge each one of you for purchasing my debut book and my devotional. Thank you for leaving reviews, watching my interviews, following me on social media, and supporting my writing efforts. Without you, there would not be an "AUTHOR TAM YVONNE," and I will be forever grateful for your love and support.

My heavenly angels, my grandparents, Mrs. Willie Alma Tate-Curtis and Mr. Samuel Curtis, Sr., I know you all are looking down and putting in good words to the

Lord on my behalf. I miss you both so very much and wish you were here to see all the magnificent things that have transpired in my life.

Lastly, but never least, the best publishing team on the planet... PEN LEGACY PUBLISHING COMPANY! You all are stuck with me as long as you'll have me. Thank you for making my childhood dream of writing books a reality. This writing journey is so much easier with you all in my corner! Thank you!

Dedication

This book is dedicated to each one of you who reached out to me to do a sequel to my debut book, *"A Leap of Faith."*

All that I put into this book is for you, and your reading pleasure. I hope that what you suggested to me has been exhibited in this sequel.

Specially, La'Toya Jones, Kimberly Terry, Krystal Garrett, Tiffany Green, Patricia Carter, Annah Clark, Versie Zanders, and Tiffany Jones for supporting my first Fans Zoom meeting and sharing your opinions about the book. As promised, I wanted to personally and publicly express my gratitude to each of you.

Lastly, thank you to my fans… "TTC" …TEAM TAM CREW…You all are the BEST!

~ ALWAYS BE A BLESSING! ~

*"The best things in life happen unexpectedly.
The best stories begin with 'and, all of a sudden…'
The best adventures were never planned as they turned
out to be. Free yourself from expectations. The best will
come when and from you least expect it."*

~The Minds Journal~

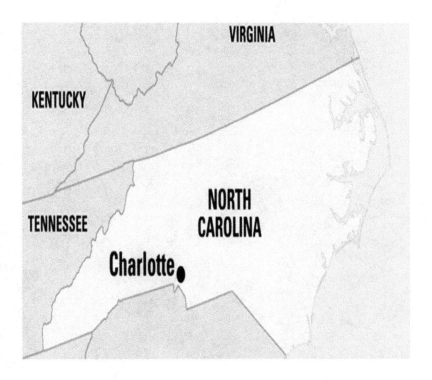

Table of Contents

Chapter 1

~Work~

"**W**ork, work, work, work, work! That's all you do, Allie," replied Leilani, Allison's best friend and Spelman College sister. "Honey, you really need to take some time for yourself. I am so very proud of this magnificent, financial president you've become with your finance company, but it's so much more to life than just working yourself silly, Sis."

"Lani, I know. But after graduate school, I have just thrown myself into becoming the best financial professional I can be, and it's certainly not left me time for anything. Heck, I barely get over to see you, my best friend, my goddaughter and Floyd and we live in the same city." Allison Gallant replied, as she typed on her office's laptop, trying to wrap up her workday at 9 p.m. in the evening.

"I understand Allie, but it's up to you. You must make time, sweetie. Life is way too short to just throw yourself into work and not enjoy the fruits of your labor. After losing daddy and having Zora, I look at life so differently now and I just want the best for you. I want you to fall in love, get married, have a baby and just not work so hard," Leilani responded.

"I know, Sis," Allison softly spoke. "I know, I will certainly try and do better. I'm not coming into the office this Sunday, so I will see you at church."

"Yaaaaaay," Leilani squealed. "Oh, my goodness... I cannot wait to see you."

Allison laughed, "I cannot wait to see you either. Well, let me wrap up this final client file, and I am getting out of here for the evening."

"Okay, be careful, and I'll see you on Sunday. Love ya, Allie."

"Love you too, Sis," Allison responded, hanging up the phone.

Allison laid back in her office chair and began to think about what her best friend had just said to her. Leilani was right; all she did was work. No time for play. She didn't even have time to fit in exercise that she enjoyed so much. She had been working hard all her life to be the best she could be, especially academically. Graduating in the top 5% of her private Christian high school in California, attending Spelman College in Atlanta, and completing her graduate degree with a 3.9 GPA at Duke University, being a high achiever was all she knew. Having a father who was a retired Superior Court judge and a big brother who was a Harvard Law grad and law professor, there was not an option to be anything but GREAT!

But who says you can't be great and still find love and raise a family? "Maybe my doctor or lawyer will show up soon," Allison laughed aloud.

All her life, Allison Gallant has been referred to as a bourgeois female because of her physical appearance and the way she carried herself. Yes, she came from a very privileged background, and her widowed father, retired Superior Court judge, Raphael Gallant saw to it that she and her brother had the absolute best, growing up in Berkeley, California. But, with her mother, Maria, dying giving birth to her, her father did what he knew was best for his children, and that was providing them with the very best of everything.

Growing up, Allison was considered "bossy," but she was a leader and not a follower. She made it her business to stand out and let anyone in her presence know that she was rich and beautiful, and many wanted to be in her circle of friends because so many people were drawn to her.

She was an attractive woman, tall and slender with light brown skin, long dark hair that she'd dye a different color in a heartbeat; dark was working for her lately. But little did they know that when she was home alone with no one around but God and her cat, Nestle, she was an insecure, scared woman who missed her mother and wanted people to love her for who she was and not what she had or who her father was.

Putting on a "game face" is all she knew. No one, except her best friend, Leilani Hamilton, knew "the real" Allison Gallant, and Leilani broke through her hard-exterior freshman year at Spelman College during an orientation and the ladies became instant friends and have been inseparable ever since.

Now, all grown up with several degrees and tons of accolades, she still did not have anyone to share her successes with. She came home nightly to a large house, fit for a family of four. The only sound was the pitter patter of Nestle's feet, jumping down from the sofa when he heard her come into the house.

She never thought her life would turn out the way it was playing out. She thought she and her college sweetheart, Jermaine Randall, would graduate college, get married and immediately raise a family. But Jermaine was not on the same sheet and had other plans. He graduated Morehouse College with a History degree and moved back to Syracuse,

New York, to attend law school, or at least that's what he would oftentimes tell Allison. He moved back to his hometown, but he married his pregnant high school sweetheart before enrolling into Syracuse University College of Law.

For four years, Jermaine played Allison and had her on an emotional rollercoaster with the hopes of them being together forever. She was willing to wait for him as long as he wanted. She had even toyed with the idea of moving to Syracuse to attend graduate school to be closer to him. But he would never be on board with her suggestions, and now she knew why. His true love was there, and he had no intentions of spending his forever with her.

It took Allison years to get over the heartbreak of being used by Jermaine, and she would oftentimes think about what a fool she was for that man and all the time she wasted on him.

Shaking the thought out of her head, Allison wrapped up her final client's file, packed her laptop up in her dark brown Maxwell-Scott luxury shoulder tote bag, grabbed her car keys, and headed to the employee parking deck.

Approaching her childhood dream car, she started the red Porsche 911 Turbo Convertible, with black lining and peanut butter-colored seats. She opened the trunk and placed her shoulder tote bag inside.

Grabbing the steering wheel, she took a deep breath, *"Lord, I know I have asked for my doctor, a man with lots of money from a wonderful background. I don't know when you are going to send me my prince, but, on this night, I ask you, whichever one of your sons you send to me, please allow me to be prepared and accepting of what you have for me. You know the desires of my heart, and I know you will only send me your absolute best. In your name, Jesus, I thank you in advance. Amen."*

Cranking her car, Allison, drove off into the Charlotte night.

Chapter 2

~Back in The Lord's House~

"Who are YOU to judge?" Leilani shouted into the microphone as the congregation yelled out their "Amen" and loud handclaps.

"That question did NOT come from me, y'all. "Do not judge! That is a command from the Lord Jesus himself. Right from his mouth in Matthew 7:1-3. I don't think you all believe me. Go to it yourselves. Turn your bibles to Matthew 7: 1-3. I don't have to read it to you; you can read it for yourself!" Leilani exclaimed.

Allison sat in her usual spot at Leilani's church on the front pew, next to Leilani's mother, Dr. Almah Mae Connor-Bassett, who moved to Charlotte after her husband, the late Bishop Ervin Bassett, passed away shortly before Leilani had baby Zora. Dr. Connor-Bassett did not want to continue living in Atlanta alone, and since retiring and at the insistence of Leilani and Floyd, more so Leilani, *"Mommy, I don't know nothing about babies."* Dr. Connor-Bassett moved into the mother-in-law suite at their home to help look after her first grandchild, Zora Nicole.

Leilani was on fire this morning. Allison was so very proud of her best friend. Leilani had always been a good minister, but she had become more confident over the past few years, and her delivery kept getting better and better. What started out as a small bible study group was now almost a megachurch in Charlotte. Leilani had really made her mark in the religious community in the Metro Charlotte area.

"I'm not going to keep you all long," Leilani continued, "but you do know judging is a sin, right? Keep on judging people. If you continue judging others, you WILL, and I repeat, you WILL be judged in the same way you judge others. Trust me. You. Will. Be. Judged!"

Taking a deep breath, she continued, "before I close, turn in your bibles one last time to Romans 2: 1-5. I am reading from the New International Version. And it reads as thus, *'You, therefore, have no excuse, you who pass judgment on someone else, for at whatever point you judge another, you are condemning yourself, because you who pass judgement do the same things. Now we know that God's judgement against those who do such things is based on truth. So, when you, a mere human being, pass judgement on them and yet do the same things, do you think you will escape God's judgement? Or do you show contempt for the riches of his kindness, forbearance, and patience, not realizing that God's kindness is intended to lead you to repentance? But because of your stubbornness and your unrepentant heart, you are storing up wrath against yourself for the day of God's wrath, when his righteous judgement will be revealed."'*

All you could hear in the church was "my, my, my," and "my Lord." Allison sat quietly, marinating on the words that had just been spoken. All her life, she'd not only been judged herself but, she had often judged others. Although she knew it was not right, hearing it just then from her friend's mouth that it was a sin to judge others sent chills over her body.

Interrupting her thoughts, Leilani spoke, "before we get out of this place. Let me close in prayer. Oh, Heavenly Father, Lord of Lords, King of all Kings, help us, Jesus! Help us to be mindful of our actions. Help us to realize that it is not our place to judge others. We are no better than they are. Lord help us to just allow You, to be You, and to trust Your plans and the transformations that You and only You can do in people. Thank You, Father God, for coming into this place, on this day to apprehend our hearts. I am coming to You today, Lord, on behalf of everyone that hears my voice, asking that You transform each soul, into souls who love unconditionally, just as You do, Father.

Help us, Jesus, to see people the way that You see people. Help us, Jesus, to show compassion, even while having wrong done to us. Help us, Jesus, to respond with love and not hate. Thank Lord for filling us with Your love and for freeing us, Jesus. YES! FREEING us from the urges to judge others. We love You, Jesus, and we thank You, Father. Father, we lift up Your name and only Your resplendent name, Amen."

The congregation responded in agreement, "Amen."

"Lani, it was so good to be back in the Lord's house today. Now that was some word today," Allison replied, rocking her beautiful goddaughter to sleep. She was sitting in a chair at her friend's kitchen table as Leilani prepared Sunday dinner. Leilani's mother had gone to take a nap before dinner, and Floyd was in his man cave watching football. Little Zora had run herself silly playing with her toys and watching cartoons before she eventually climbed into her 'Aunt Allie's' lap and fell asleep.

The little girl had grown so much in the past year and was a mixture of both Leilani and Floyd. Beautiful, smooth brown skin like her dad, big bright eyes like her Mom, and a head full of thick, black hair that Leilani kept in two big ponytails.

As Allison stroked the little girl's cheeks, she began to speak, "I really needed that message today, Lani. All my life, I have been judged, and I learned to judge others the way they were judging me. I think I've actually missed out on some good relationships because the men didn't come in the package that I wanted them to come in. All my life, I have been so set on marrying a doctor or an attorney. I just can't see myself with anyone less than that. Am I wrong for that?"

Looking up from the pot she was stirring, Leilani responded, "you're not wrong at all for wanting the best for yourself, Allie. But sometimes, what we want for ourselves, the Lord doesn't want that for us. That is why we should allow Him to find our mate and ask Him to give us the strength and know-how to be able to handle and deal with what HE sends to us. You know as well as I that what He sends to us is going to be more than we could ever imagine, and girl, that's whether the man is a doctor, lawyer, trash man, or cook. If he is God's son, honey chile, you already know he'll step to you right. He'll act right. He'll be right. He'll do you right, and you'll know it's right. No second-guessing. No insecurities, none of it."

Allison sighed, "I know you're right. I've truly been trying to work on myself. But I know I'm still a work in progress."

Leilani laughed, "Amen to that."

"What?!" Allison laughed.

"No," Leilani chuckled. "I was joking. Trust me, we are all still a work in progress. Just because I'm married, and a prophetess doesn't mean I don't have things to work on. Because I do… a whole lot!"

Leilani placed the salmon in the oven and walked over to sit in the chair across from her friend.

"So, what are your Christmas plans this year? Are you going to see your dad in California?"

"Well, that was the plan, but daddy has decided to go to Innisbrook Golf Resort in Palm Harbor, Florida, to do some golfing with his retired buddies, and Novak has a new girlfriend, so he will be in Connecticut meeting her family for the first time. No plans for me. I may take Nestle into the office with me and knock out some things before the end of the year and be all fresh and ready for the new year," Allison replied.

Leilani felt sorry for her friend. She knew Allison had been so in love with Jermaine in college and really had her hopes up to marry him after college. He had left without any warning and moved back to his hometown and married his high school sweetheart. Although she didn't talk about it much, Leilani knew that Allison thought about it often, which made her somewhat bitter. The reason she threw herself into her work all these years was her way of coping with the loss of that relationship.

As 18-year-olds at Spelman College, she knew Allison was not the snooty person she had tried to be. It was a wall she had put up to not let a lot of people get close to her. After all, who wanted to deal with a stuck-up person all the time? Not many people, but Leilani, with her loving spirit, broke down that wall and won Allison over. They had been best friends ever since.

"Well, promise me you'll drop by here for Christmas dinner with us," Leilani replied.

"Now that I can do," Allison laughed.

Getting up, Leilani picked Zora up from Allison's lap, "let me take sleeping beauty to her room."

Allison kissed the little girl and handed her over to her mother.

"Maybe one day," she thought. *"Maybe I'll get an opportunity to be a Mommy, too."*

~Lord, Who Is This Man?~

The winter season had finally kicked in, and that North Carolina winter weather was no joke. Allison was bundled in her coat, scarf, hat, boots, and gloves as she ran into the office building.

"Good Morning, Jon," she greeted the security officer at the front desk.

"Good Morning, Miss Gallant," smiled an older white gentleman with red hair. "Is it cold enough for you?"

Shivering, Allison responded, "oh boy! It certainly is. Growing up in California and going to college in Atlanta, I never had to deal with this type of winter until I moved to North Carolina. Cold is an understatement."

The older gentleman laughed. "Miss Gallant, I was just informed that for the next month or so, we will have a new cleaning team coming in to clean the building."

"What happened to the old team?" Allison asked.

"I don't know the details, but to my understanding, there was a disagreement with the owners of the building, and they are out the door," Jon whispered as if to be sharing a secret.

"Well, I appreciate you letting me know, Jon. Because I am usually here late, and it would've startled me to see some new faces. Good looking out, my friend," Allison smiled.

"Anything for you, pretty lady," Jon smiled back.

Allison nodded and headed toward the elevators to get to her office on the 14th floor.

"Mr. Clements, it has been a pleasure having you as a customer. It appears that your portfolio is doing very nicely, and everything is in order. I greatly appreciate you giving me the opportunity to handle your finances."

Allison wrapped up her phone call with her client just as her cell phone began to ring.

"Hello."

"Hey, Allie girl, what's going on?" asked her best friend.

"Nothing much, Lani. Busy, busy, busy," Allison replied.

"Same here. I just wanted to reach out since we didn't get a chance to do our daily morning chats. Time just really got away from me."

"I know, and the weather isn't the best."

"Tell me about it. I'm working from home today. I'm surprised you tackled that weather and went in," Leilani responded.

"It was a beast, but I had to come in. I had a 9 a.m. call with one of my clients and his file was here in the office. Trust me; if I could've pulled it up from home, I would've been in my PJs all day," Allison laughed.

"Well, I have mine on, and it's grrrrrrrrrrrreat," Leilani laughed. "Well, don't stay too late tonight, Allison. I just wanted to check on you."

"Aww, aren't you the greatest, best friend in the world," Allison teased.

"Girl, hush," Leilani laughed.

"No, seriously, I'll be fine. I won't be here too long tonight. I hear it's going to get rough."

"Right. So, leave early. Love ya, girl."

"Love you too, Lani," Allison replied, hanging up the phone.

"Excuse me, Miss," a deep voice startled Allison as she was focused on the documents she was reading before her.

Allison jumped and turned around to find a tall, very dark skin bearded man standing in her doorway.

"I'm sorry, Miss. I didn't mean to startle you," he continued.

"How can I help you?" Allison asked, disregarding his statement.

"I'm Ronald McMurray with McMurray's Cleaning Services," he introduced himself. "We're new to cleaning this building, and I wanted to come in and clean your space if it's okay."

Staring at the man before her in her snobby way, she pointed towards the trash and turned back around to her computer.

Coming into the office, Ronald shook his head and shrugged his shoulders, thinking, *"another educated, independent stuck-up woman."*

He dumped her trash and placed her trash can back in its location. "Have a nice day, Miss."

Not turning around, Allison threw up her hand.

"Hmmm, he doesn't look anything like Mr. Wallace," she thought. Thinking about the tall, slender, dark skin bearded chocolate man that just came into her office. It had been a long time since she had taken notice of a man, and even though the new custodian wasn't Idris Elba fine, he wasn't too bad looking, especially since all she worked around were old, gray headed white businessmen every day. Occasionally she'd run into some attractive young black men when she was on a different floor, in the lobby, or on the elevator. Still, it never became anything but a quick "hello."

"Who was that man? He had to be at least six feet two", she thought with very smooth, dark brown skin and a jet-black beard. He appeared to be bald-headed, but she couldn't fully tell because of the company hat he was wearing, and after all, she wasn't going to be gawking at some trash guy coming to clean her office.

Shaking her head and pulling herself together, she gathered the paper on her desk, placed it in her shoulder tote, looked at the clock on her wall displaying 6:30 p.m.

"Let me get out of here before I get snowed in," she thought and headed for the door; she was starving and wanted to hit her favorite soul food restaurant before she got home to grab a veggie plate for dinner.

It was colder outside than it was that morning because the sun had gone down. Winter had truly arrived in the Queen City.

Chapter 4

~Miss Snippy~

For the past two weeks, he had been working in Allison's building, "Ronald" would politely knock on her door daily, greet her, empty her trash and wipe down her office. All the while being ignored by the snooty woman who often had her back turned to him. By this time, she knew his routine and made it her business to have her back turned so she wouldn't have to conversate with "the help."

Ronald was used to educated, professional women, ignoring him and not thinking he was *good enough* to breathe the same air as them. But, for some reason, as snobbish as she tried to be, there was something about the lady he finally learned was named *"Miss Gallant."* He couldn't quite put his finger on it, but, in his heart of hearts, he did not think she was as pompous as she had tried to portray.

Earlier in the week, he found out from some of the other maintenance guys in the building that she was a very successful finance professional who drove a *"bad"* meaning good Porsche. She lived in a beautiful home out in Davidson. The fellas had already done their homework on her, but they also told him that she *"thought she was all that."* The fellas had informed him that she did not talk to anyone in that building if they weren't on *"her level."* They had labeled her *"Miss Snippy,"* because they said any time you said *"hello"* to her, sometimes she might mumble a *"hello"* back, but most of the time, she ignored you.

As much as he wanted a serious, committed relationship, he certainly didn't want one with a rude, curt woman who looked down on others. He had dealt with an adulterous, ostentatious wife for fifteen years and certainly didn't want to go through any more hardship in a relationship. He was just going to wait on God, raise his daughter and make his money.

Even though not impressed with anything that *"Miss Snippy"* had materially, there was still something about her spirit that continued to capture his curiosity, and he wasn't going to stop until his interest was fed.

"Lord," he thought. *"If I'm to learn more about 'Miss Snippy,' I mean, 'Miss Gallant,' please align everything the way in which you want, and I will follow."*

Chapter 5

~You Gotta Eat~

"Girl, I cannot believe this!" Allison whined. "We are snowed in."

"I told you not to work so late. Allie, it's eight at night, and you're stuck in an office building. Who else is there?" Leilani asked.

"I'm the only one on my floor. Security's on the bottom level, and I think there are a few others in the building. I thought I heard that janitor guy fumbling around here earlier," Allison replied.

"What janitor guy?" Leilani asked. "What happened to Mr. Wallace?"

"According to the security officer, Jon, Mr. Wallace got into it with the owners of the building, and they let him, and his company go. They voided the contract and ended up going with another company. Now we have this new company. A guy with a company called *'McMurray Cleaning Services.'*"

"Young guy, hmmm," Leilani replied.

"Girl, please. He doesn't appear that young. I guess a little older than us," Allison replied.

"Is he cute?" Leilani asked.

"I don't know," Allison replied. "I guess for the janitor type."

"SEE! I have told you, Allison Maria Gallant!" Leilani exclaimed. "Didn't I just do a sermon on judgmental people, and here you go with your judgmental ways."

Allison was quiet for a moment. "I'm not trying to judge, but he's not my type, okay."

"I didn't ask you all of that, Allison. I asked was he cute. A yes or no answer," Leilani snapped back, "and you jump in bougie mode talking about you guess for the janitor type. What's the janitor type?"

"Lani, c'mon, now. I get it. I shouldn't have been judging the guy," Allison replied. "My bad."

"But since you said it. What is the janitor type?" Leilani asked again.

Laying her head back on her chair, Allison sighed, "he's cute, Lani. Okay, I said it. He ain't Idris, but he is tall, slender, dark, bearded nice teeth… I guess he is attractive in his own way. But I could never."

Allison could picture her friend on the other end of the telephone shaking her head in disapproval, "There you go again. You are so set in your ways. You are going to have to get out of your own way, Allie, or you're going to forever be searching for something or someone that may never come around and, in the meantime, missing out on blessings that are crossing your path," Leilani told her friend. "I'm not going to preach to you," she continued, "but you're my best friend, and I just want you to be more open with others and allow yourself to learn all kinds of people. Just because someone isn't from your same background doesn't mean that they are not good people. God's children come in all different kinds of packages. Quit sticking to the packages, you know. The lakes and the rivers you're used to and allow God to deliver some different things to you."

Allison closed her eyes and thought about the words that just came out of her friend's mouth.

"I've said my piece," Leilani continued. "I love you. You know that, and I'm not trying to be your mom or jump down your throat. I just want you to think about some things. You be safe up there, and please let me know when they say it's safe for you all to leave. Okay, Allie?"

"Okay, Lani. Love you, too," Allison responded, hanging up her phone.

Just then, Ronald stuck his head in her doorway with a large brown bag in hand.

"Have you had dinner?" He asked.

Lifting her head, she saw the tall man standing in her doorway, with a smile on his face, holding up two bags.

"I knew I would be coming in and that it was a strong possibility I might get stuck here for a few hours, so I grabbed myself some dinner and got extra just in case you were around and hadn't had dinner. You're welcomed to it if you like, Miss Gallant," he continued.

Staring at the man, she cleared her throat. "No, I don't think so. But thank you, Mr. McMurray, right?"

"You can call me Ronald, and I insist," he replied, stepping closer and placing the bag in front of her. "It's a grilled chicken salad from my favorite restaurant out in Concord; you're going to love it."

"Thank you," Allison smiled. "Very thoughtful of you."

Turning around heading back to the door, Allison called after him, "where are you eating?"

"I was going to go back to the janitor's closet and listen to some music and enjoy this great salad," he smiled.

"You're welcomed to eat here," Allison smiled slightly, pointing to the chair in front of her desk. "If you don't mind, could you close my door?"

Ronald closed her door and took a seat in front of her desk.

Pulling out two bottled waters from the small refrigerator on the side of her desk, she handed him a bottle.

"Thank you," he replied.

"You're welcome."

The two ate in silence for a moment, then Ronald broke the silence. "Are you from North Carolina?"

"I am not. I grew up outside of San Francisco, California," Allison replied.

"A Cali girl," Ronald smiled. "I'm from Alabama. A small town outside of Auburn."

Allison smiled. *"So that's where the accent comes from,"* she thought.

"Auburn. Yes, I've been down there twice for football games," she replied.

"War Eagles," Ronald chanted. "I was born and raised in Alabama. I'm the youngest of four boys. My mama was a stay-at-home mom, and my daddy worked at the iron plant in Montgomery, Alabama. We didn't have much, but we had a lot of love. Very rich with love."

"How nice," Allison smiled, sipping on her water. "My mother died giving birth to me."

Looking up from his salad, Ronald replied, "oh my goodness. I'm so sorry, Miss Gallant."

"Please call me Allison, and it's okay. I have an amazing dad who took on both roles. But I often think it would've been nice to have a mom growing up."

The two continued to eat in silence until Allison's office phone rang.

"This is Allison Gallant. Hi, Jon…" she began.

Sitting in silence and looking at the pretty lady in front of him, Ronald felt there was something special about her and wanted to learn more.

Hanging up her phone, she replied, "we can now go home. That was Jon, the security officer. They've gotten the *go ahead*."

"Great! I need to get up and wrap up the other offices, and I'm out of here," Ronald replied, packing up his trash.

"Thank you again for dinner," Allison responded, balling up her trash and throwing it in the trash can. "You were right. The salad was very good."

"It was my pleasure, Allison," Ronald smiled, walking out of her office.

Chapter 6

~I Don't Know~

"Lani, I don't know," Allison spoke into her cell phone, laying across her bed. "I have taken your advice and started getting out of my own way and just allowing 'things to happen... but...'"

"But what, Allison?"

"But I don't know," Allison groaned. "It's like unexpected things are beginning to happen."

"That's how God works, Allie, and it's just a date. I'm quite sure it took every bit of courage in him to ask your snooty butt out on a date," Leilani laughed.

Laughing back, Allison replied, "now you know you're wrong for that, and I'm not all that snooty."

Both ladies began laughing.

"It just seems like after we got snowed in and had dinner in my office, I started wanting to know more about him, even though he's not the type I'd typically date," Allison rejoined the conversation.

"It's not about what you typically date, Allie. It's about how you feel when you're in his presence, and you two haven't gone out or been in one another's presence outside of that office building, so this might be a good thing. You'll actually get to see him outside of that work uniform and possibly see him as a MAN… and not as the 'janitor type' as you call it."

Pondering, Allison replied, "you're right. What will it hurt to go on a date with him, right?"

"Right."

"Enjoy it and bring all the details back to me," Leilani laughed.

"Later, girl."

"Later."

Chapter 7

~First Date~

"Wow, you look amazing," Ronald replied as Allison let him into her house. Allison had on a black one-shoulder top, and a gray front slit belted skirt with a pair of black suede Sam Edelman Hazel stilettos.

"Thanks," Allison smiled bashfully. She knew she was looking good in her outfit. Her nails and toes were done, and her hair was fierce.

"As pretty as you are, I hate to tell you, you're going to have to change," Ronald began.

"Change?" a puzzled Allison asked. "Why?"

"Because where I'm taking you, you need to have on a pair of jeans," Ronald smiled.

"Jeans?" Allison questioned with a weird look on her face. All the work she had just put into herself and this man was standing before her telling her she needed to go and put on a pair of JEANS?! "Our first date, and I have to wear jeans?"

"Trust me. It'll be fun."

"I don't know, Ronald. Maybe we should just call this thing off. I'm not a big *'jeans'* person, and I thought we were going to go someplace to get to know one another, like *Fleming's,* for a few glasses of wine and great steaks. *'Fun'* isn't what I had in mind. Plus, I don't wear jeans like that anyhow. I may have like three pairs of jeans."

"So, you're telling me, you can't just go throw on a pair of jeans and a top?" Ronald questioned.

Bewildered, Allison replied, "hold up, Ronald McMurray. What do you mean 'throw on'? I don't throw on anything. I put my ensemble together with plenty of thought and care… I don't just throw on clothes," Allison snapped.

Holding up his hands as if to defend himself, Ronald chuckled, "don't bite my head off. Please don't take what I say so literally."

"I'm glad you find this funny. But I've never been asked out for a first date, and the date included jeans," Allison retorted.

"Can you please just trust me, Allison?" Ronald requested. "I promise you it'll be a fun time for all."

Puzzled, Allison thought about what he just said, *"fun time for all."*

"I know good, and well, we are not double dating with people I don't know for our first date," she silently thought. *"Okay, Allie, suck it up, go and make this the first and last date with this tacky joker who has no class."*

"Okay, Ronald. Whatever. I'll change," Allison finally spoke up. "Give me a few minutes. Have a seat."

Ronald sat down on her dark brown, L-shaped sofa in her family room, and began watching the cooking program she had on the screen.

Minutes later, Allison returned back to the family room, where Ronald was sitting, wearing a pair of black Ted Baker skinny jeans, a white fitted Breton top, a black double-breasted pocket side coat, a pair of black and white "Chucks" and a set of real pearls she received from her father for her 21st birthday years ago.

Ronald jumped up as she entered the room. Keeping his cool, he couldn't believe how beautiful she was, even in jeans… with her arrogant self.

"Now that's more like it," he teased, clapping his hands together.

Rolling her eyes and interrupting his bantering, Allison spoke, "so, where are we going?"

"It's a surprise," he answered. "I do have one stop before we get to our destination if that's okay."

Allison nodded, "let's go."

They rode in silence the entire ride, listening to the gospel singer Smokie Norful's song, *"I Need You"*.

"This is one of my favorite CD's," Ronald broke the silence.

"Yes, Smokie is an amazing singer," Allison agreed.

"Allison, there is something I want to tell you," Ronald began.

Allison looked over at the man driving. "Yes, what is it?"

"I'll understand if you decide not to see me again," he continued. "But I... umm..."

Allison's heart began to beat fast. *"Oh, my Lord,"* she thought. *"I've let my guard down, and this joker probably has a whole wife and five babies."*

"I'm umm," he stammered.

"Spit it out," Allison exclaimed. "What is it?"

Looking over at her for a brief second, he responded, "I'm a single father."

"So, you have children?"

"I have a child. A ten-year-old daughter named Ronalda who I am raising on my own."

Ronald pulled into a parking spot in front of the local ice-skating rink.

He stopped speaking for a moment and looked over at Allison, who was looking straight ahead.

"So, when were you going to tell me you had a child?" She finally asked.

"I mean, I just didn't know the right time," he mumbled. "Work wasn't the right place to share, and I thought if I got lucky enough to take you on a date, that I would get an opportunity to share that information with you."

"Hmmmm," Allison slowly responded, nodding her head. "So, what other secrets do you have, Mr. McMurray?"

"Ronalda isn't a secret, Allison. She's my daughter, and I just didn't know how to tell you," Ronald spoke. "I was married for fifteen years, and my ex-wife, Sandra, left Ronalda and me for her supervisor, with who she was having an affair for years."

"Oh, Wow! An ex-wife, too," Allison dramatically responded.

Ronald continued, "Sandra, my ex-wife said that I wasn't big time enough for her. That I was cramping her style, and when she got pregnant with Ronalda, she made it plain as day that Ronalda was my baby because she didn't want any children in the first place and especially not any children with me. So, she left us a 'Dear John' letter and moved to Tennessee with her boss. I tried to stay in Alabama and continue working, but coming from a small town, I was embarrassed. Everyone knew my business, Ronalda was getting teased in school, and things just weren't going right. That's when I decided to leave Alabama all together and start over some place, I knew nothing about."

"One day, I was sitting in my kitchen with an Atlas in front of me, watching Ronalda eat her breakfast. I opened the map. North Carolina was the first page I turned to, and I asked Ronalda to point to anywhere on the page, and she pointed to *Charlotte,* and off we went… leaving what we knew in Alabama and starting anew here in Charlotte," he explained.

"I'm sorry to hear all of that, but don't you think that's something you should have shared with me before you even asked me out on a date? At least give me an option to decide if I want to deal with a man who's been married before and has a child?" Allison questioned. "I've never been married, and I don't have any children, and I prefer to date men who have never been married and have no kids. I want to experience those firsts for the first time with someone who will be as excited as I will be. You already know how marriage works. You know how it feels to become a father for the first time. IF… and that's a big IF this would have gone any further, that excitement wouldn't have been there for you."

Feeling the chill in the car, Ronald sat silently before finally saying, "Firstly, it's funny how there are two brains in this car, but one is thinking and speaking for the both of us."

Allison rolled her eyes and continued looking straight out of the window.

"I do understand, Allison, but you cannot tell me how I would feel to remarry and have more children. That is a bridge that has to be crossed when I get there. Just because someone has experienced some life experiences does not mean that it was done correctly and that all enthusiasm is gone and can never come back," he enlightened.

Starring at the pretty lady not giving him eye contact, he continued, "I appreciate you accepting this date invitation. I should have been more forthright before asking for any of your time outside of work."

Crossing her legs, Allison began getting uncomfortable. "Why are we here? I don't ice skate."

"I'm here to pick up my daughter. Her ice-skating lesson is over," Ronald cautiously whispered.

"Oh my gosh, you cannot be serious, Ronald! You're going to introduce me to your daughter? We barely know one another. Isn't that rushing things a bit?"

"I didn't think it would do any harm, and I'm a package deal. I'm new here. I have no one to watch her, and I wanted to take you out. I have to balance my life, and in order for me to get to know someone, my dates have to revolve around the fact that I'm a father first. I don't date a lot, and I try not to introduce Ronalda to a lot of different women."

Allison rolled her eyes and began to shake her head. *"Never again,"* she thought. *"I honestly cannot believe my life has come to me dating men who are 'package deals.'"*

"I'll be back," Ronald spoke, getting out of the car and going into the building. Watching him walk up the entrance to the rink, Allison had to admit, with his southern twang and all, there was something about that man… but was she willing to find out what?

Moments later, Ronald returned with a pretty little brown skin girl, with sparkly, bright brown eyes and long cornrows in her hair.

"Ronalda, this is Miss Allison," Ronald introduced.

Getting in the back seat of his black Honda Accord LX 4 door Sedan, the little girl greeted Allison, "hi, Miss Allison."

"Hello," Allison managed to smile.

Ronald got into the driver's seat and began the vehicle.

"Daddy, where are we going?" Ronalda asked.

"Well, Miss Allison has been kind enough to hang out with us this afternoon, so I wanted us to do something fun together. So, we are heading to the Arcade!"

The little girl squealed with excitement! "I just love the arcade!! Don't you, Miss Allison?"

Allison could not believe what she was hearing. This man had her change her clothes. Informed her that he was married to an adulterer and on top of that he was the father of a 10-year-old little girl... not to mention, for their first date, he's taking her to an Arcade, as if they were fifteen years old.

"Am I being punked?" Allison thought. *"This cannot be happening to me right now. Oh, my Lord, I hope I do not see anyone I know. What are you talking about, girl? You won't see anyone you know... because people you know don't hang out at ARCADES!"*

"I haven't been to an arcade since I was a kid," Allison sarcastically responded to the little girl, all the while looking over at Ronald, who was concentrating on the road. "But I'm sure it'll be fun for you and your daddy."

Ronald looked over at Allison, ignoring her disdain. "Well, this will be your opportunity to relive your youth and enjoy some air hockey, skeeball, arcade games and bowling."

Ronald paid the fee for himself and the ladies to get into the arcade, which had a restaurant. Walking behind

Ronald and his daughter with her arms folded, Allison walked over to the bar inside of the arcade restaurant.

"A glass of *Château Pape Clément*, please."

"A glass of what?" A confused young man asked from behind the bar.

"Do you all have *Château Pape Clément*?"

"Ma'am, I have no clue what that is."

Allison responded, breathing heavily and getting annoyed, "what types of red wines do you have?"

"We have one type," the young man responded.

"Annnnnd that is?" Allison asked.

"Roscato Rosso Dolce."

"Give me a glass," Allison demanded.

As she was getting ready to pay for her glass of wine, Ronald came up behind her and paid the bartender.

"I had that," Allison spoke sharply.

"I know you did, but I insist," Ronald answered, ignoring her bad attitude. "Ronalda and I have a table over by the window. We'll have lunch before we start playing games."

Allison followed him to the table with wine in hand, where the little girl was sitting.

"You can sit by me, Miss Allison," the little girl smiled, patting the space next to her.

Reluctantly Allison sat down by the grinning little girl. Allison managed to put a fake smile on her face. All she wanted to do was enjoy her cheap glass of wine, eat cheap bar food and go home and never think about this first date ever again.

The young man from the bar walked over. "We are short staffed today, so I'll be your waiter, too."

"Go figure," Allison thought.

"What will you folks be having?"

"Chicken tenders and French fries," Ronalda spoke up. "And a Sprite to drink."

"And you ma'am?" The young man asked, looking at Allison.

"I'll have the grilled chicken, spinach, and garlic butter rice."

"And you, sir?"

"Let me get the giant party cheeseburger with all the fixins', French fries, and a root beer."

"Woooooooooooow!! That's a big burger, daddy," Ronalda laughed.

"I'm a big guy," Ronald teased the little girl.

"That was yummy!" Ronalda exclaimed.

"It was good," Allison agreed, having loosened up a little after her second glass of wine.

"Well, ladies, let's go have some FUN!" Ronald exclaimed.

The party of three played various video games, bowling, and miniature golf. Ronalda found another little girl that she began playing games with as Allison and Ronald took a break at one of the tables nearby, watching the kids.

"Allison, I'm sorry for springing all of that information on you at once."

Allison stared at the man in front of her. He wasn't bad looking, and he smelled so good. Not the kind of man she'd typically date, but he was attractive in that hard-working, manly kind of way.

"You did what you thought was best," she replied.

"It has been so hard for me to find someone who's willing to accept me first and secondly my daughter. I haven't dated much since the divorce because I don't want to introduce Ronalda to a lot of women and risk her getting attached, and the relationship doesn't work. She's at an impressionable age, and I know she misses her mother. I just can't put her through anything else. Or myself."

"So, you're looking for a mother for her?"

"I didn't say that Allison. Please don't twist my words."

"So, what are you saying?"

"What I am saying is that. I'm not dating just to be dating. I loved being married. I love the idea of being one woman's man. I am a Christian, and I'm not ashamed to say that. I don't believe in having multiple women. My parents didn't raise me that way. My father, who I admire so much, wasn't that type of man to my mother, and I wasn't that type of man to my ex-wife either. When God blesses me with my forever wife, I won't be that type of man to her," Ronald explained.

Staring at the man in front of her, Allison had never met a man who felt so strongly about his faith and wasn't uncomfortable to share his beliefs so lucidly.

Ronald continued, "I'm no preacher, and I don't claim to be. But I do know that Titus 1:6 states that *'an elder must live a blameless life. He must be faithful to his wife, and his children must be believers who don't have a reputation for being wild or rebellious.'* My father was that type of man. That's what I saw, that's what I know, and that's who I am. None of my siblings were out of control or rebellious. So, I'm trying to live a 'do right' life, so Ronalda and my future children will do the same."

Quite impressed, Allison smiled at the man before her. "Your faith is very important to you, isn't it?"

"Miss Allison, my faith is everything to me," Ronald smiled back.

Just then, Ronalda ran over to where they were sitting.

"Hi, sweet pea. Where's your friend?"

"She had to go."

"Oh, okay… well, it's time for us to go, too," Ronald smiled, kissing his daughter on the forehead.

They all got up and headed to the parking lot, Ronalda jumping on her father's back for a piggyback ride to the car.

Pulling up in front of Allison's home, Ronald looked at the sleeping little girl in the back seat. She had had a long day with her ice-skating lesson and games at the arcade.

"Let me walk you to the front door."

"No, I'm good, Ronald. Thank you for the afternoon. Get your daughter home; she's had a long day," Allison replied, getting out of the car and walking up her driveway.

She knew she could have been less high and mighty throughout the day but dating a janitor with a ten-year-old child was not in the plans she had for her life, and she didn't want to "settle." After all, she was a successful business-woman, the president of her own financial firm; with a lot to offer, she needed someone who could provide the same or more.

The next morning Allison went into the office and had two messages on her office phone from Leilani, in addition, to the many text messages her best friend had been sending.

She closed her office door and called her friend back.

"Where have you been?" Her concerned friend asked. "I have been texting your phone, calling your office phone… nothing. Are you okay? Was your date that amazing that you had to rest up before calling me back with the details?"

"Girl, nothing amazing about it. I just needed to go to sleep. I had consumed two glasses of wine, and you know I can't really drink, so I was absolutely done for the night," Allison elucidated.

"What do you mean nothing amazing? Was it that bad?"

"It wasn't the best. Girl, that joker is divorced with a 10-year-old daughter!"

"He just told you that?"

"Yes! The day of our first date, and on top of that, we ended up going to get his daughter, who went on the date with us. Sweet little girl, but…"

"Oh, Wow! What was his reasoning for procrastinating with that information?"

"He said he didn't know how to share that information with me. So, his brilliant idea was to share on our first date. Trust me when I tell you, that was the first and last date with that guy. If he withheld that information, what else is he withholding?"

"I understand your dismay, Allie. But give him the benefit of the doubt. He may not be covering up anything else," Leilani spoke softly. "I've been your best friend a long time, and I know that you can be quite intimidating. So, it's probably true he did not know how to break that news to you, and with the little girl being present, it probably made it easier and more comfortable for him to share all of that information. Because most people don't go off in front of children."

There was a brief silence, and Leilani continued, "And besides, what did I tell you about judging?"

"Lani, I'm not judging. I just don't want to date a blue-collar man with a child. What's wrong with that? Aren't I entitled to having preferences?"

"I didn't say you couldn't have preferences, Allie; I was just saying, quit judging that man for the type of work he does. Every time you refer to him, it always has to do with him being a working-class man. Now that you found out he gave his heart to a woman he felt was marriage material and started a family, you see an issue with that. How was he supposed to know the one he gave his heart to was going to tear up his marriage and leave him with a little girl to raise on his own?

"But..." Allison began.

"There's no but, my friend. His story happens to plenty of good people, whether it's a man or a woman. Everyone isn't out here just dating to be dating and casually having sex with people. There are a lot of men out here seeking a wife and who want to be a father. Do you know how many single men in my ministry schedule meetings with me just to talk about such? I thought you told me that's the type of man you wanted. Someone who wants to be married and have a family?"

"I do want that, but I just prefer someone who's never been married and doesn't have any children."

"Stipulations. Allison, there are always conditions with you. I get what you're saying, but sometimes it doesn't work out under your terms. You don't know what God has in store for you and what God's provisos are for your life. You don't know whose life you're going to change or who is going to change your life. Have you ever thought about that?"

Allison remained silent, holding the phone, like a child being reprimanded for getting out of hand with a parent.

Interrupting her thoughts, Leilani continued, "I surely hope you weren't arrogant. I know how supercilious you can get at times, Allison Gallant!"

"I know you didn't," Allison managed to laugh. "I am not supercilious!"

"I didn't say you were, but you can be at times, and I can talk to you this way because I'm your best friend, and I know you, and I know how snobbish acting you can be," Leilani kidded.

"Lani, get out of here. I don't try to be. I'm just who I am."

"No, but seriously, Allie. As your friend, as your sister, I truly think you need to get out of your own way so you can find the love you deserve before you get too old, and the pickings are slim to none," Leilani laughed. "You're already successful and happy for the most part, all you're missing is love, and you are standing in your own way, hindering yourself from obtaining what God has in store for you," Leilani spoke unequivocally.

Thinking about her conduct the other afternoon, Allison had to admit that she was anything but hospitable and her demeanor was quite humbug.

"I mean, I guess I could've been more sociable."

"I hope you weren't callous to the little girl because you were in your feelings, Allison."

"Oh no... absolutely not. I'm not that unpleasant, Lani," Allison defended herself.

"Good. So, what are you going to do?"

"I'm not going to do anything, Lani. It's over. Even if I did apologize, I'm quite sure he thinks I'm this uppity, self-centered woman, and the energy he had for me will not be the same."

"From what you say about him being a Christian man. I seriously doubt he'll allow you and your ways to interfere with the feelings and the energy he was feeling towards you."

"No, I'm good, Lani. I'm going to ignore him as much as I can. Plus, I have this huge deal on the table at work that I need to focus on, and if I make this happen, I will be a very wealthy woman."

"Okay, Allison, whatever you decide, I have your back. I hear Zora crying in her room. Let me go check on her. Mommy has gone to the supermarket with Floyd, so we'll talk later. But now is the time for you to repent and go into deep prayer and ask God for forgiveness and for Him to let His will be done in this situation."

"I can't argue with that, Lani. Kiss my god baby for me."

"You know I will. Love ya, Sis."

"Love ya back."

Chapter 8

~Get Out Your Own Way~

I t had been over a week since Ronald had asked and took her out on their first date. After he had dropped her off at home, Allison had not heard a word from him, and somewhere in the back of her mind, she was hoping that she would. *"But why would he reach out to someone who complained and found fault with the entire afternoon,"* Allison thought. *"Maybe Leilani was right. Maybe I was getting in my own way from finding love. After all, the white-collar, professional men I had been dating all these years, not one wanted to commit to just one woman. Their mindset was 'the more, the merrier'. They wanted to brag and boast about their careers, cars, money, houses, clothes, etc. Not one that crossed her path wanted to date monogamously. Always casually, and here, out of nowhere, appears a man, not just any man, but a man of God who was not afraid to admit that he loved and lost. That he wanted only one woman and to raise his daughter to be a good human being. And what do I do? I act all superiorly because I did not have any kids and had never been married as if that was a good thing. At least Ronald knew what love was... I didn't!*

Every day he looks into his daughter's eyes, he is blessed to know what it is to love someone more than himself."

"What a nincompoop!" Allison exclaimed aloud, turning her head to look out of her office window at the snow falling. *"You really know how to mess things up, girl."*

Before she knew it, she was dialing his number on her cell phone, but it went directly to his voicemail. *"Oh my. He's blocked my number,"* she thought, with tears welling up in her eyes. *But she had no one to blame but herself and her own actions,* she thought.

Laying her cell phone down on the desk, Allison spoke aloud, *"Dear God, please take this critical spirit away from me. I know that behavior is a learned behavior and can be corrected. Judging others is not who I am. I repent. I know I have fallen short. I have judged without understanding. Please, Father God, this day, fill my heart with compassion and help me not to condemn but to seek first to forgive. Help me, oh God, not to judge. Amen."*

Before she knew it, tears were running down her face. Grabbing a Kleenex, she wiped her eyes. *"I don't want to be alone."*

Chapter 9

~Where Is He?~

Allison had been calling and texting Ronald for the past week with no success until she finally gave up. She was beginning to look obsessive and desperate. She was concerned about him because he had not been coming into the office, but her trash was getting emptied. Maybe he just decided not to do her floor any longer and allowed one of his workers to do so after hours. She didn't know because she hadn't had any communication with him, since the evening he dropped her off at home; and the late hours she'd been working, she no longer had to, after landing the huge deal with a major client she was working on.

Just then, there was a knock at her office door.

"Come in."

"Good Morning, ma'am, may I empty your trash?" asked a short, full-figured Latina woman.

"Sure," Allison replied.

Walking over to her trash can, the woman began doing her job.

"Excuse me, are you with McMurray's Cleaning Service?" Allison asked.

Looking up, the woman responded with her slight Latin accent, "yes, ma'am. I work for Mr. McMurray."

"Would you happen to know where Mr. McMurray is?" Allison enquired.

"Yes, ma'am. Mr. McMurray's mother died. He is in Alabama," the woman spoke sadly. "She had a stroke."

"Oh, my goodness," Allison exclaimed. "Thank you."

"Yes, ma'am," the woman nodded and left Allison's office, closing the door behind her.

"That is why she had not heard from him," Allison thought. *"Oh my God! I have to get in touch with him."*

Picking up her cell phone once again, Allison dialed Ronald's number, and just as she was about to hang up, she heard his velvety, manly voice, "hey there."

"Ronald, hi," Allison managed to say.

"I'm sorry about not responding to your calls," he jumped in, explaining.

"Oh, no need for apologies; I just heard about your mother, and I am so sorry."

"Thanks. Ronalda and I are here in Alabama. There is so much to get in order, and my dad just isn't in the right state of mind right now to handle this on his own."

"I can only imagine," Allison responded. "Is there anything I can do?"

"No. But thank you."

There was an awkward silence for a moment, and Allison expressed, "I'm sorry, Ronald."

"I know," he responded.

"No, I mean about the date thing," Allison tried to clear up.

"I know," he responded again.

"You know?"

"Yes. We're from two different worlds, Allison. You're this woman who was born with a silver spoon, and I'm the total opposite. Just a country boy from the State of Alabama who has worked hard for everything he has. Why would someone like you want to give someone like me a chance?"

Feeling terrible listening to his words, Allison tried to interject, "it's not like…"

Interrupting, Ronald continued, "I thought about what you said, and you're right. You do need someone who hasn't experienced the experiences I have. You deserve that. You worked hard for that—someone on your level. The only thing I have to offer to any woman is unconditional love, protection, honesty, trust, communication, patience, kindness, empathy, and compassion. I'm not the richest man, but I work hard, and I love harder."

Tears were coming down her cheeks; Allison didn't know what to say. She had never had any man come into her life and express himself so eloquently, and these were men with two and three degrees.

"I am glad our path crossed, Miss Allison, and I wish nothing but the best for you."

"Ronald…"

Just then, Allison heard Ronalda in the background, "daddy, come here. Granddaddy wants you."

"Allison, I have to go, but I wish nothing but the best for you, and I pray you find what you're looking for. God bless you, pretty lady," Ronald replied, hanging up the phone.

Sitting bewildered and heartbroken, Allison cried like she never had. God had sent her the man she needed in her life. Not in the package she wanted nor expected, and she let it get away… all because she couldn't get out of her own way.

"Dear God, please give me a second chance," she weeped.

Chapter 10

~I Blew It~

Speaking through tears, Allison sat across from her best friend, "Lani, what goes around certainly comes back around."

The two ladies were in Allison's family room, with the fireplace going and the soft tune of a James Taylor, 70s Lite Rock song playing on the satellite radio.

"Girl, I thought I had done everything right. Boy was I wrong. Amid trying to climb the corporate ladder, getting dumped without warning by Jermaine, I never found time for love and when I did let my guard down and attempt to date again, I always ended up with men who didn't see me as anything but a trophy girlfriend. Someone to show off to their homeboys, family and friends."

Wiping her tears, Allison continued, "they didn't care a bit about my feelings, what I wanted in life. My desires to become a wife and a mother. All they saw was this rich, pretty, Spelman College educated woman, who they could dress up and parade around town. Ronald did not care about any of that. He got me out the stilettos and into the Chucks. He wanted to humble me, and that's what I have been missing in my life. Humility, and he brought that, along with his strong Christian values. I am such a fool."

"You are far from a fool. You're a human being, and as humans, we make mistakes. It's natural. If it's meant to be, it will be," Leilani comforted her friend.

"Lani, I blew it before it even got started. I truly believe he is the one that has gotten away. It really sucks to be me right now," Allison wept.

"Allie, Ronald is a man of God. He has a lot on him right now. He just lost his mother, and he has feelings and emotions all over the place. Give him some time. I can promise you one thing. He was feeling you, and I don't think he's going to let what he was trying to accomplish go that easily."

Looking up at her friend with tears in her eyes, Allison replied, "do you really think so?"

"I do think so, Allison. You just watch and see," Leilani responded, reaching over and giving her friend a huge hug.

Leilani couldn't believe that her friend was finally coming around. God does answer prayers. For years she had prayed for God to remove the critical spirit she saw in her friend, many years prior when they were college students, and although it did not happen right away, she truly believed God's will was being done now. A change had come for Miss Allison Maria Gallant, and unfortunately, it took heartbreak to get there, but nonetheless, change was emerging… and it was a beautiful thing.

"What a mighty God we serve," Leilani thought. *"His timing. Not ours."*

Chapter 11

~I Had No Right~

Allison studied her reflection in the wall-sized mirror in her walk-in closet, searching for shadow and bags under her eyes and any other telltale signs of her sleep loss. She'd gotten up early to put her makeup on heavily because she had not been looking like her usual put together self. All things considered, she supposed she looked suitable for the office.

Considering her recent heartbreak, her company was having their annual Christmas party. She wanted to at least appear merry, so she wore her merriest Christmas outfit— a red plaid sweater dress that seemed to look like a two-piece but was a one-piece zip on dress with a mock neck and flirty flounce hem skirt showing off her sleek silhouette. Her long dark hair was curled and hanging in the center of her back with a side part. Although she had been down in the dumps, she was still Allison Gallant and did not want to give the impression that she had been slogging around in the agony of despair.

"The set-up is so nice," replied a short, plump lady.

"It really is pretty in here," Allison responded to the lead Paralegal in her office. "Who decorated?"

"To my understanding, an outside vendor was called in. I think the company's name is *All About Christmas,* and they have done a stunning job," the woman smiled.

The annual Christmas party was a big deal, and each year it kept getting better and better. This year's theme was *A White Christmas,* and the auditorium was gorgeous. There was a live band, live lilies all around, paper origami birds, snowflakes, and everything was dusted with spray-snow. Absolutely heavenly.

Just as Allison was heading over to the hors d'oeuvres table to grab a bite and a drink, she spotted Ronald walking into the room. Her heart skipped a beat. She had not seen him in weeks, and he appeared in the doorway like a knight in shining armor. He was wearing a classic fit Fairisle Quarter-Zip white sweater and a pair of gray dress pants.

Just as she was preparing to turn away, their eyes met, and he started walking in her direction, showing those perfectly aligned white teeth.

Getting nervous, she exhaled, telling herself to just breathe. She did not need to go into a full-blown panic attack in the middle of the party.

"There you are, Allison," Ronald replied, walking over and standing in front of her, all six feet two of him.

Managing a smile, Allison responded, "Here I am. I am here."

"I had stopped by your office to see if you were going to be coming down here to the party, and here you are," Ronald continued. "I got back in town a few days ago. I stayed in Alabama longer than I had intended, and Ronalda ended up staying with my dad to keep him company. She'll return when her Christmas break is over."

Allison smiled. She was so nervous she didn't know what to say. She didn't know if Ronald was just making small talk or if he was really glad to see her at the party. She didn't know how to respond to him, and that was not in her nature. *What was it about this man? It had to be the God in him.*

"So, what do they have good here to eat? I'm starved," Ronald responded, grabbing a plate and placing the appetizers on his plate.

Giving up hope of fleeing, Allison grabbed a plate and started selecting the appetizers she wanted to eat. Once both of their plates were full and beverages in hand, Allison walked over to a table in the back corner of the auditorium, Ronald following close behind.

Allison had not taken a bite of her food and just blurted, "I'm sorry! I had no right to judge you, Ronald."

Holding up his hand, Ronald asked gently, "Is that what's bugging you? Because I was expecting a better welcome back than I just got," he smiled. "Didn't you miss me as much as I missed you?"

"Yes, I've missed you terribly, but I have felt crappy ever since that day, and when we finally spoke, you basically wished me the best, and that was it," Allison responded with tears welling up in her eyes. "I thought I'd never see you again."

"Did you really think I was going to give up on trying to win you that easily?" Ronald questioned.

Looking up in his big brown eyes, Allison's long-lashed eyes lifted to meet his. "I honestly thought it was over before it actually started."

Ronald rubbed her cheek. "Trust me, my love. Nothing is over. We are just beginning."

Allison blinked and managed a soft smile. "I'm glad." With a sense of wonder, she lifted her hand and reached out to touch the side of his face.

"So, are you good now? I never want to see another tear unless it's tears of joy," he spoke in a calm voice. Without giving her a chance to say anything, he added, "You are wearing that dress, Miss Gallant."

Allison's heart somersaulted at his compliment and at his fragrant scent and the light touch of his hand as he moved hers from his face and held both of her hands with his in front of them at the table.

Trying to get her bearings together, just the thought of having this sweet man in her life was beyond her comprehension, but she was willing and ready for all that came with finding out what life with Ronald McMurray was like.

Chapter 12

~Dinner and a Movie~

Ronald eyed Allison's practically untouched dinner plate. "Is something wrong with your dinner? Now I know I'm not the best cook in the world, but it can't be that bad," he joked.

She looked up. "Oh my gosh, no! This New York strip is excellent, cooked to perfection. Scrumptious meal."

"I don't know about that, pretty lady. You sure haven't eaten much of it, and since this is our first date without child, I wanted this to be a special date for you."

Jabbing at her baked potato, Allison ordered herself to begin eating. "I'm so sorry, my dear Ronny. Today was such a busy day at work. I guess I'm a little beat. But I didn't want to just go home and not get an opportunity to end my day on a good note by spending some time with you."

Ronald's mouth turned up into a smile. "Well, your evening will be less stressful for sure, Miss Gallant."

Ronald's words sent a chill gushing through Allison. Ever since the office Christmas party, their attraction to one another had intensified, and Allison had been experiencing thoughts about her man that she had not thought about any man for many years. After her toxic relationship with Jermaine, she knew that she wanted to wait until marriage before she was sexually involved with anyone again. She couldn't help but shudder at the thought of her and Ronald making love for the first time, and she tried not to think too hard or allow a full picture of her thoughts to develop. But just the thought of their bodies entwined left her speechless.

"I can't believe you're going to watch a chick flick with me," Allison joshed.

Sitting closely on the sofa, Ronald looked at the woman next to him with a crooked smile and twinkle in his eye, "Why not? I'd watch any movie just to spend time with you because I'm really fond of you, and I'm not going to lie; I love being near you."

Allison tugged on her long ponytail. For some reason, this man-made her so shy. A characteristic she never had.

Shyness was never in her vocabulary. She could not bring herself to meet his gaze.

Sitting back on the sofa, they continued watching the movie. Suddenly, Ronald grabbed her feet and began massaging them with his warm hands. "After a tough day, my Queen needs to relax."

Throwing her head back slightly, Allison spoke, "Gee, that feels nice. I have not had my feet massaged in such a long time."

He smiled. "So, tell me. How was it growing up in sunny California?"

Allison took a deep breath. "I think I briefly shared with you that my mother died during childbirth, having me, and after that, it was just my daddy, big brother Novak and little ol' me."

She swallowed and moistened her lips, "Daddy was a Superior Court judge. He's retired now and is enjoying traveling the country. He was very involved with my brother and me and saw that we had the best of everything. He truly was a mother and a father to us. The three of us took care of one another."

Allison couldn't help but smile, thinking about her amazing father. The tall, slender, dark man who had always been her hero. "He was a very busy man with his career, but he never let that get in the way, and I loved that about him. We came before everything, and that's why I adore him so much."

"Did you miss not having a mother around?"

Allison paused to consider the question. "I may have at times, but daddy left no room for that. Plus, I had three aunties, his sisters who lived less than thirty minutes from us, and they were very protective of their little brother and helped him look after us."

"So, did you date a lot?"

"In high school, I was quite popular, and I had a lot of acquaintances, but no boyfriends in high school. Plus, I was a nerd. Everything was academics, cheerleading, church, and my chores at home, in addition to cooking and cleaning at our house, even though we had a maid. My daddy wasn't playing that mess. We still had chores. I had no time to date or really socialize, and my daddy was very strict about dating."

Giggling as she recollected. "I can recall when I finally grew into my womanhood and left California for Atlanta, Georgia, to attend Spelman College. I… um… fell hard for this sophomore at Morehouse College. Jermaine, who I dated my entire college career. I shared the news with my daddy and when he visited for parents' weekend, do you know that man took two hours and gave me an entire sex education course. He had printed pictures, was using the medical terminology and all."

Ronald and Allison both laughed.

"So, what happened with you and Jermaine?"

With a lump in her throat, Allison took a deep breath and began. "After he graduated Morehouse, a year before I finished Spelman, instead of staying in Atlanta like we'd agreed and discussed for four years, he moved back to Syracuse, New York, where he was from. At the time, I didn't know why he had made the impulsive decision to move back to New York. But I later found out that he was engaged to his high school sweetheart, and she was expecting their first child."

Allison felt a sob building and tried to suppress it. After all, she knew she was over Jermaine, but just the thought of the emotional rollercoaster he had her on for four years of her life always made her melancholy.

Before she knew it, she was weeping in Ronald's arms, with her face buried in his chest.

"My sweet Allison. I'm so sorry," Ronald whispered as he rubbed her head. "I shouldn't have meddled."

"I'm sorry for crying. Trust me, I am over him," Allison sobbed.

"I know you are, baby. Go ahead and cry. Get it all out because this will be the last time you cry over another man. It was his loss and my gain."

Allison put her arms around his neck and hung on to him and the gentleness he was offering to her. "I'm okay," she said, getting her crying under control. "It's been years now since all of that. I'm acting like such a juvenile." Before she knew it, she was nestling into his warmness.

"You're far from a juvenile, Allison. You're a woman who gave her all to love and was hurt in the process," his hands journeyed lightly over her back.

Allison could feel his heart beating gradually, and she placed her hand on his chest. His heartbeat sped up the moment she touched his chest, and she snatched her hand away. He grabbed her hand and placed it back over his heart and held it there.

She raised her head to look at him. "Thank you," she mouthed.

He brought her hand up to his lips and kissed her palm. Allison immediately felt a pulsating deep in her core. She knew she should leave because she didn't want to do something she'd regret later, but she also knew she had no strength to move. Just then, he moved her hand to his cheek, and they gazed at one another.

Allison could see the hunger in his eyes as he lowered his head and placed his mouth on top of hers.

His mouth was open, and he gently licked her lower lip with his tongue. She gasped. Never had she ever been kissed in such a way. She parted her lips, and he plunged in with his tongue, exploring the moist and soft inner parts of her mouth.

They embraced one another in a smoldering, sensual kiss. Ronald was giving a lot, and Allison reciprocated with enthusiasm. She melted in his arms as his hands cupped her breast. She moved her hands to caress his neck.

"No sex before marriage, "she thought. But the feelings going through her body were saying otherwise. She had made a promise—no sex before marriage. But like in the cartoons, there was an angel on one shoulder and a little devil on the other. She had to fight the temptation, even though it felt so right being in his arms, pleasuring him, and being pleasured by him.

She loosened her hold on him, and he slowly pulled away. "As much as I'd like to continue this, Ronald…"

He put his finger to her lips.

She blinked. "But—"

"Trust me, baby. I know. We both know where this is headed, and it is best we stop now, or we won't be able to." He stood up from the sofa.

"In due time."

"This man is perfect. I got to be dreaming," Allison thought.

Chapter 13

~Didn't See It Coming~

"So, I finally get to meet your best friend?" Ronald replied, looking in the mirror and fixing his red and white Santa hat that matched the one Allison was wearing.

"Yes. Leilani and Floyd wanted us to come over for a small Christmas gathering that they are throwing at their home. You also get to meet my precious goddaughter, Zora. Ronny, she is the most precious little thing, and she's learned to walk, so she's all over the place," Allison laughed.

"I can't wait," Ronald smiled.

"Ronald, welcome to our home," Leilani smiled, handing him a glass of wine. "We have heard so much about you. It is so nice to meet you finally."

Allison and Ronald were the first guests at the Hamilton's home, and Leilani and Floyd were thrilled to meet the man that humbled, the oh so bougie Allison Gallant.

"Yes, we are, man," Floyd chimed in. "I was beginning to wonder about my sister here."

Lightly punching Floyd's arm, Allison laughed, "whatever, Floyd! I'm not that bad."

The couples began to laugh aloud.

"It's nice to meet you all, too," Ronald replied in his southern accent. "Allison talks about you guys all the time."

Just then, the doorbell rang; and Allison and Ronald walked over to sit on the sofa facing the burning fireplace.

Leilani and Floyd had such a beautiful ranch style home. Very comfy and cozy, like something out of a southern homes' magazine.

"Heeeeeeey, girl!" shouted a loud female voice.

Allison immediately recognized the voice. It was Deniece Mitchell. A mutual friend of her and Leilani's and a church member of Leilani's ministry.

Deniece was a fun and pretty woman around their age. She was from the Charlotte area. She walked in looking as beautiful as ever with her white fur coat and black leather heel boots. She always had on heels. Allison didn't know if it was because she was only five feet tall, or she just liked heels. Behind her was her husband of over twenty years, Michael Mitchell. Michael was quite a bit older than Deniece and such a pleasant man.

Standing up, Allison replied, "heeeeeey, Deniece!"

"Oh, my goodness, Allison! Hey girl," Deniece exclaimed, running over to give Allison a hug. "Now, this is a surprise! I did not expect to see you. I thought you'd be working. I have not seen you in months."

"I know. I have had so much going on," Allison smiled, hugging the cute, short lady.

Getting up, Ronald stood behind Allison.

Tilting her head and biting her bottom lip, Deniece continued, "umm… okaaaaay. I see you have been busy."

Laughing, Allison shook her head. "Deniece, you are a true mess. This is my love, Ronald. Ronald, this is Deniece and her husband Michael is the guy hanging up their coats."

Extending his hand, Ronald greeted the woman. "Nice to meet you."

"Nice to meet you, too," Deniece smiled.

Deniece's husband, Michael, joined the conversation.

"Hi. I'm Michael," he replied, extending his hand to Ronald.

"Nice to meet you, man," Ronald greeted.

"Hey there, Allison," Michael replied, hugging Allison.

"Hey, Mike. Good to see you."

All the couples found places to sit between the living area and the dining room. Leilani spoke, "no one in this house is a stranger, so the kitchen is set up with drinks and food; help yourself. I'm not making anyone's plate but my hubby's and mine. So, if you're hungry, you better do it yourself."

Laughing, the ladies got up and went into the kitchen to make plates for their men and themselves.

"He seems so sweet," Deniece began the conversation.

Smiling, Allison responded, "he is, and to think I almost messed up my chances with him."

"You what?!" Deniece exclaimed.

"It's a long story, girl. I'll have to catch you up one day," Allison said, shaking her head. "Not today."

Laughing, Deniece replied, "that chocolate kiss is something nice."

"Oh, my goodness, Deniece," Leilani voiced, shaking her head.

"What?!" Deniece asked. "I know I'm happily married, and my Michael is my everything. But I'm not dead, and I have eyes. I know a good man when I see one and Allison; his spirit is beautiful. I feel it and just the way he stands near you and looks down at you. He got it bad for you."

Taking a deep breath, Allison professed, "ladies, I'm in love."

Both Leilani and Deniece started jumping up and down, clapping their hands like schoolgirls who just found out their friend got asked out by a popular boy.

"Oh my, Allie. That is wonderful," Leilani uttered, hugging her friend. "This holiday season is going to be the absolute best!"

Just as she spoke, her doorbell rang.

Grinning harder, she said, let me go get that.

Allison couldn't recall her best friend saying more people were going to be coming over, so she continued fixing her and Ronald's plate. As she was preparing to walk into the living room, she heard a familiar voice. "There's my baby girl."

She looked up, and her dad and brother were standing in the kitchen's doorway.

"Oh my GOD!!! Daddddddddddy!" Allison exclaimed, running and hugging her father tightly. The two embraced for what seemed like forever before her brother, Novak, spoke up, "uh uh, you have a brother, too."

"Novak! Hi," by this time, Allison was in tears, hugging her brother.

Getting her bearings together and wiping her eyes, she looked over at Leilani. "How in the world did you pull this off?"

Smiling, Leilani responded, "Novak and I had touched base, and I told him that I wanted to do something special for you for Christmas. But what do you get someone who has everything? And because you hadn't seen your father and brother in a while, I thought it would be a good idea to invite them here for the Christmas gathering. Novak was in Chapel Hill, North Carolina anyhow, meeting friends before heading up to Connecticut, so he agreed to drive down, and when he called your father and told him what I was trying to do, your father said one day from playing golf with friends wasn't going to hurt anything. He had to see his 'baby.' So, he took a flight, Novak picked him up from the airport and TADA!"

"Oh my God! This is the BEST gift ever," Allison smiled, hugging her father again. She felt like the five-year-old little girl who loved when her father picked her up from kindergarten class.

By this time, the men had joined everyone in the kitchen. Leilani and Deniece introduced their husbands, and Allison summoned for Ronald to come over to where she was standing with her father.

"Daddy, this is my love, Ronald. Ronald McMurray," Allison smiled, grabbing Ronald's hand.

"Nice to meet you, Sir," Ronald replied a little nervously.

Starring at the man before him. Judge Gallant didn't speak quickly. The room fell silent as everyone was awaiting the elderly man's next move.

Getting nervous, Allison examined her father's facial expression. Finally, the judge spoke, "so, you're the reason for this here glow I see on my baby's face?"

Breathing a sigh of relief, everyone in the room started laughing and smiling.

"Yes, Sir. I am," Ronald responded.

"Well, it's a pleasure to meet you too, son," the elderly gentleman extended his hand, and they both shook hands.

Allison's brother Novak introduced himself, and he and Ronald greeted one another.

"Everything was so delicious," Deniece declared.

"Yes, it was," Leilani's mother expressed. She had joined the guests after her and Zora's afternoon nap.

Zora was toddling around and eventually ended up sitting on Allison's lap. Ronald and Allison were playing with the toddler girl, making her giggle.

"This has truly been a wonderful evening, and I just wanted to go around the room and have each of us express what we're thankful for," Leilani began. "I would first like to thank our Lord and Savior for bringing all of us together this holiday season. I know that each of us live very busy lives, but making time for loved ones is the best. I greatly appreciate each of you for taking time out of your lives to fellowship with my family and me. I am so blessed to have each of you in my life. I am so blessed and thankful for my wonderful husband, Floyd, my beautiful baby girl, Zora, and my loving mother. I don't know what my life would be without you all."

Floyd smiled at his wife and continued, "as my wife stated, it truly is a blessing to have great friends who are more like family, and I am pleased that you all are in our lives, and my man, Ronald, welcome to the family. I am thankful for my beautiful wife, my baby girl, my mother-in-love, and my extended family."

"I'm thankful for life, and all of you," Leilani's mother jumped in.

"I'm thankful for my Michael, our children, you all and all the blessings God has bestowed upon me," Deniece grinned.

"I'm thankful for my Deniece," Michael spoke up, putting his arms around his wife. "Our children and good health. Thank you, Lord."

"I'm thankful for this moment—this time to be back with my children, Allison and Novak, in the same room. I am thankful that my other daughter, Leilani, blessed us with this moment. I am thankful for life and good health, and lastly, I am thankful to know that my daughter is in good hands here in North Carolina," Judge Gallant replied, looking over at Ronald with a smirk.

"I am thankful for everything you all have said, and I just want to wish us all more happiness, not just now but for years to come," Novak spoke up.

By this time, everyone was looking over at Allison and Ronald.

Clearing her throat and handing Zora over to Leilani, Allison responded, "I'm thankful for my family, my friends, my career, my health." Pausing, she looked up at Ronald staring down at her. She continued, "and second chances."

Giving her a side hug, Ronald spoke up, "Amen to second chances. I, too, am grateful for second chances. My daughter, Ronalda. My health. My business. My new friends and my future wife."

By this time, Ronald was bending down on one knee in front of Allison. The room was so quiet you could hear a pin drop.

Leilani immediately started crying tears of joy for her best friend.

Allison gasped. She could not believe what was happening.

"Allison, I was planning to propose to you later tonight, but this just seems like a better and more memorable opportunity, especially since your father and brother are here,"

Ronald began. "I know we've only been dating a very short while, but it doesn't take months, years, or a lifetime to know what you want, and I know that I want you in my life forever. I want to grow old with you. I want to raise a family with you. I want to protect and take care of you. After losing my mother, I had an epiphany. Life really is short, and tomorrow isn't promised. I want what my parents had—fifty years of marital bliss. As long as I have you and Ronalda in my life, I'll be a happy man. But at this moment right now, you would make me the happiest man on the planet if you say you'll be Mrs. Ronald McMurray."

Tipping her head back to keep from crying, Allison looked back down at him on one knee. She loved to look at him and his amicable face. He always shook her up, and this moment was no exception. She couldn't think straight, and all eyes were on her.

Clearing her throat, she began, "are you sure? I mean…"

As she rambled on, Ronald's cool expression glanced up at her. "Allison, I can assure you I have never been surer in my entire life."

Allison could hear someone behind her say, "awww."

"I want you in my life forever. We almost lost one another, and I will not allow that to happen again."

"I'm crazy about you, and YESSSSS!!!!" Allison bellowed.

Placing the two-carat shimmering diamond pear-shaped solitaire engagement ring on her finger, Ronald stood up, and the two kissed.

Everyone cheered. Deniece and Leilani grabbed Allison's hand to see the ring, and all three ladies squealed and hugged.

"I didn't see all of this coming," Allison replied excitedly. "This is the best Christmas ever!"

Chapter 14

~Sweet Home Alabama~

"Dad, we're here," Ronald yelled as he and Allison got out of the car onto a red dirt road on his father's farm in Alabama.

Allison had agreed to ride down to his hometown on the outskirts of Auburn, Alabama, to pick up Ronalda since Christmas break would be ending. She needed to get back to Charlotte to prepare for the second semester of school.

The front screen door of a modest tiny two-story home with a large front porch opened, and a tall, jovial man appeared in the doorway. "C'mon up. I have been dying to meet Miss Allison."

Walking up the steps, the man was now standing on the porch.

"Hi," Allison smiled.

"Hi, beautiful," the elderly man greeted, reaching down hugging her. "You sure are pretty."

Smiling, Allison replied, "thank you."

"How did you pull this one off, son?" The elderly man joked.

"I don't know, Dad," Ronald laughed. "God had favor."

Just then, Ronalda came running out the door. "Daddy... Allison!"

Picking her up, Ronald hugged his daughter. "Hi precious! You've been taking care of granddaddy?"

"Yup."

"She sure has. Such a little lady," the elder McMurray responded. "She's become quite the little cook."

"Hi Ronalda," Allison smiled, rubbing the girl's back, who was still in her dad's arms.

Putting her down, Ronald replied, "Ro, we have something to tell you."

Looking up at them both, the little girl smiled, "what?"

"Daddy has asked Miss Allison to marry him."

Waiting for the little girl's expression, Allison smiled nervously.

Rocking in his rocking chair, the elder McMurray watched as the situation played out.

Finally, the little girl spoke up, "I get my very own Mommy?!"

Allison's heart melted, and she thought, "*Oh my gosh. What a sweet child and to think I was willing to throw all of this unpretentious love away.*"

Before Ronald could answer, Allison answered back, "yes, sweetie. You will have your very own 'Mommy' who will love you lots!"

The three hugged as the elder McMurray smiled. "*I think he found the one his soul loves,*" he thought, looking up at the sky, where he believed his dear, sweet Mildred was resting safely in God's arms.

Knowing how his late wife worried about her sons, the senior McMurray smiled and whispered, "*Mildred, I do believe our boy is going to be alright.*"

Chapter 15

~By the Power Vested in Me~

"And now, by the power vested in me by God and the state of North Carolina, I pronounce you husband and wife."

Prophetess Leilani Hamilton grinned with gratification as she looked from Allison to Ronald. "You may now kiss your beautiful bride, Ronald."

Smiling broadly, Ronald put his arms around Allison's waist, pulled her to him, and planted a long kiss upon her smiling lips. On the beautiful Saturday morning, the guests inside the church all burst into applause to express their endorsement of this union.

Allison's father, who was seated on the front row, dabbed at his eyes, thinking, *"if only her mother were here to see how beautiful of a bride her baby girl was."*

The violinist began to play a cover song, *"You Are the Reason,"* that Allison selected to accompany them when she and Ronald walked together down the aisle for the first time as *"husband and wife."*

"You look beautiful, my Queen," Ronald smiled down at her as they walked the aisle.

Sweeping past their guests, both glowing with so much love and happiness, Allison smiled. "And you look handsome, my King."

"An entire week alone. Just you and me," Allison said.

"Yes, my beauty. A week of Mr. and Mrs. Ronald McMurray," Ronald smiled, looking away from the road in front and pulling one hand from the steering wheel and patting his jacket's breast pocket. "Airline tickets right here. Jamaica, here we come!"

Allison giggled. "Ronalda sure was excited to get back to her granddaddy, wasn't she?" she asked. Ronalda wanted to go back to Alabama and help with her grandfather while the two were away on their honeymoon. "She sure was," Ronald answered.

As much as Ronald wanted a longer honeymoon with his new bride, as an entrepreneur and father, one week was all he could manage. But he promised his wife that they would take frequent vacations and mini getaways as often as they could.

Allison could not wait to be in paradise with her King. Seven glorious nights in Jamaica, a tropical paradise. She settled contentedly in the passenger seat, ready for the honeymoon to begin.

She and Ronald had talked about starting a family, and they both agreed that they were ready and, as Ronald would say, *"if it happens, it happens."*

And Allison knew without a doubt that having a baby with Ronald was certainly something she had dreamed about all of her life. She watched the passing landscape, thinking not long ago she almost lost the man of her dreams because of her judgmental ways and worrying about what others would think if she ended up with someone who was not *"on her level."* But GOD allowed her best friend to be a true friend and be as real as she could with her, informing her to get out of her own way and allow GOD to do his job.

Allison shook her head. *"It is amazing how GOD steps in when you let go and let Him do what He has in store for you,"* she thought.

Looking over at his wife, Ronald could see she was in deep thought. "You good, babe?"

Turning to smile at her husband, "I couldn't be better. I am so happy."

His smile made her heart flip. "I'm glad," he whispered. "Because I plan on spending the rest of my life making you happy."

"Wow," Allison thought blissfully. This feeling felt like a romance movie. She could see the title, *Miss Snippy Finally Finds Love.*

Chapter 16

~A Bug?~

Sitting at her desk, Allison had been eating on saltine crackers and drinking hot Green tea all morning. About three weeks after she and Ronald returned from Jamaica, she had been feeling a little icky, and now her appetite was limited to crackers and hot tea.

"Allie, are you there?"

Leilani was on her office speakerphone. "I'm here," Allison spoke up.

"I know what's going on, and you do, too."

Reaching for another cracker, Allison nibbled on the corner. "Girl, it's a bug going around. I am fine. I'll get over this in a few days."

"Honey, this has been going on for weeks. This is not a bug, Allison Gallant McMurray. You have been sick every morning. Not able to hold food down, and you have not had your period."

Allison stared out her window, looking at the Charlotte skyline. She knew she was pregnant. She had secretly taken a pregnancy test the other night and had not shared the news with anyone. She knew she could no longer deny what was happening inside of her body.

Speaking slowly, she asked her friend, "I don't know if I'm ready to be a mom. Am I ready to be a mom? What if I do something wrong? I don't have a mom to call and get advice. You have Dr. Almah."

"Allie, you absolutely are ready to be a mom, and you are going to be a great mom."

"I am so scared," Allison replied with tears filling her eyes.

"You know as well as I that Ronald is going to be overjoyed. The way that man loves you and to know you all created that bundle of joy growing in your stomach. Girl, get out your feelings," Leilani laughed.

Rubbing her stomach, Allison moaned, "I guess you are right."

"Let me know how it goes after you tell him. I need to get ready to head over to the church," Leilani responded. "Love you."

"Love you, too," Allison replied, taking her friend off of speakerphone.

Leaning slightly back in her office chair, Allison could not help but think about the very first time she and Ronald made love. It was on their wedding night. Allison had never seen Ronald so passionate. He prolonged each moment by slowing down his passion to savor the sweet glory before him. His hands were gentle; his mouth searched, his body was hard and satisfying.

Neither one of them had the strength to move after, and Allison remembered snuggling against him, with her hand over his fast-beating heart. She was delightfully worn out and could not think clearly, but she was with the love of her life, the one GOD had for her, and besides, it was their wedding night; she did not need to think clearly.

She traced her fingertips languorously over his damp chest, his arms, and his stomach. She eventually fell asleep, caressing him.

That next morning, she remembered feeling lazy, complacent, and heavenly. She snuggled under the blanket, lifting the blanket to her nose to smell Ronald's lingering scent, evoking pleasant memories of the night before.

Interrupting her daydream, the timer on her cell phone went off. Allison glanced at the clock on her wall and tugged on her long, dark ponytail. She truly felt like crap. *"Dear Lord, please let these hormones get under control,"* she prayed as she got up and prepared to meet her husband for lunch at their favorite Italian restaurant.

Looking out her office window at the cloudless blue sky and rubbing her stomach, she was going to be a MOMMY! She could not believe she was pregnant. The new life growing inside of her was part of Ronald, and she was so ready to pour all of her love onto him… or her … the baby.

Sighing deeply and talking down to her stomach, "I guess you will be here in the fall, my precious baby."

Chapter 17

~Our Family~

Allison grabbed her grey Goyard 'St. Louis' tote bag from the car passenger seat beside her. She looked in her car mirror at her reflection. She managed to pull herself together and must admit she looked pretty darn good for a saltine cracker eating, tea drinking, pregnant woman. She had taken her hair out of the ponytail and brushed her long dark tresses and parted it down the center. Looking like a young version of her mother, her hair fell down to the center of her back. She looked down at the royal blue and black; round neck chain printed belted dress she was wearing. Thank goodness her stomach was not showing because the fitted dress clinched every curve of her body, she thought. She loved the royal blue color of the dress, it reminded her of her and Leilani's sorority color, and royal blue was always flattering on her.

Touching up her pink lip gloss and giving herself one last glance over, Allison grabbed her purse, flipped her hair, and took a deep breath. She breathed a panicky prayer, swallowed hard, and climbed out of her car.

Waiting by the hostess stand, Allison spotted her tall, dark and lovely husband. Allison stared at him, thinking what a lucky woman she was to have such a kind-hearted, loving, Christian man in her life.

"Hey there, good-looking," he smiled, bending down to kiss his wife.

"Hi," Allison smiled back.

Following the hostess to their table in the restaurant's private corner, they took their seat at the candle lit table.

"Babe, no wine?" Ronald asked. "That's so not you."

Wishing she could have a glass of red wine, Allison murmured, "I can't."

"Speak up, babe. I didn't hear you."

Speaking up, Allison replied, "I can't, baby."

Staring at his wife with concern, Ronald asked, "Why not? Do you not feel well?"

Allison thought now was a better time than ever to lay the news on Ronald that he was going to be a father… again.

Allison forced herself not to look away from her concerned husband's gaze. She felt as if he could see right through her. At that moment, she felt so naked.

"There is something I have to tell you," she began in a soft voice, praying that her voice would not start shaking.

Ronald saw the seriousness on his wife's face and grabbed her hand from across the table.

"I have been trying to figure out for weeks how to tell you… that you are going to be a father again, Ronny."

Ronald let out his breath, and his hand rubbed her hand.

"I knew those boobs were getting full," he joked, getting up from the table and sitting beside his wife, cradling her in his strong arms.

Allison pulled back slightly to look at his reaction. There was a sparkle of a tear in his eye.

"A baby!" He exclaimed.

His exhilaration reassured her, but she wanted to be sure and asked, "Are you okay with that?"

"Okay? Oh, you beautiful specimen of a woman… okay, is an understatement. I love being a father to Ronalda and to be blessed to get the opportunity to be a father to another son or daughter and to have you as my child's mother; I am more than okay. I am blessed!" Ronald stroked her stomach with his unsteady fingers. "Allison, my angel,

I fell in love with you a long time ago and wanted you to be my wife and mother of my children. But I could not admit any of that to myself because I did not know how you felt about me, and I did not want to go through what I went through in my first marriage. I have always wanted my own family. Just like my parents and here we are now… building our family."

Allison felt his words tingle through her body. *"Our family."*

"I thank God I did not let my fear keep me from pursuing you."

Allison kissed his cheek, "and I am glad that my snooty attitude did not keep me from finding the man of my dreams and building my family… our family."

Our family. What a beautiful ring to it… *The McMurray Family.*

He rubbed her stomach and bent down to place a lingering kiss on his wife's lips. Ronald's heart melted at the touch of her lips on his. For the first time in his adult life, he felt all of his fears go away. They no longer mattered because with the love he saw in his wife's eyes, he knew he had nothing to fear with that woman of God by his side.

A warm sea of pleasure engulfed both Allison and Ronald, and she tilted her head up towards him. Cupping her chin and tipping her face up, he replied, "As long as I have breath in my body, I will always love you and our babies."

"And I'll always love you."

His mouth covered hers.

They returned home that evening and spent the remainder of their evening demonstrating their love for each other.

•

Chapter 18

~A Feeling Like No Other~

"Can I hold him?" Ronalda asked, reaching for her new baby brother.

"Sit on the sofa," Ronald motioned his daughter. Walking over to where the little girl was sitting, he placed a beautiful, caramel colored baby boy in her arms.

"Ohhhhh, he's so cuuuuute," the little girl squealed.

Smiling and sitting next to the child, Allison looked up at Ronald, who was still standing in front of the sofa.

"You did so good," Ronald smiled down at his wife and rubbing her head.

"So, did you," Allison laughed. "I don't know what I would have done if you weren't in that delivery room with me."

"Alijah Ronald McMurray," Ronald smile. "My boy!"

The excitement that Ronald had in the delivery room when the doctor told him and Allison, they had just had a boy child did not go away. He finally had a namesake. A male child he could raise to be a good, Christian man.

"Baby, I have never had a feeling like the one I had when I brought Alijah into this world," Allison began. "It was like an out-of-body experience and to think that our amazing God allowed this little sweet pea to grow for nine months, and once he was done, he came and so perfectly."

Sitting beside his wife on the sofa, Ronald hugged her. "It is truly amazing what God does."

Interrupting their conversation, Allison's cell phone rang. "Hi, Lani."

Putting her on speaker, she continued, "thank you so much for all of the dinners you and Dr. Almah prepared for us. I won't have to cook for at least a week."

"Yes, Sis! Thanks," Ronald chimed in.

"You all are so welcome. How is my nephew? You know I cannot wait to get over there and get my hands on that beautiful baby boy."

"He is good. Sitting up here being held by his big sister," Allison smiled, looking down at the doting big sister, rubbing her brother's cheek.

"Wonderful. I won't hold you all long. I just wanted to check-in. You get some rest, Allie."

"Love you, Lani. I will."

"Love you, too."

Allison had finally finished breastfeeding and putting Alijah to sleep, and Ronald got Ronalda all tucked away in bed. They could both catch their breath and spend some quality time alone together before going to sleep and having to get up and do it all over again.

"Come lay with me, Allison," Ronald replied, patting her side of the bed.

Lying beside him, she laid her head on his chest.

"Thank you," he continued.

"For what?"

"For giving me, my son. You are my sweet, sweet angel," he replied, stroking her hair.

She snuggled closer to him, and he bent down and kissed her forehead. She lifted her face to his and looped her arms around his neck, and he pressed his body against hers. "I love you," he said.

"And I love you," she whispered. *My Lord, I cannot believe you've blessed me with all of this happiness that I have been missing for so long*, she thought. *The feelings I've been feeling are like none I have ever felt, and I thank you, Lord.*

Interposing on her thoughts, Ronald's hands encompassed her waist, and his grip tightened. "I know we can't do anything just yet. You're still healing, but the little I can do, which is kiss and touch you, I plan to do tonight. I have to have you, my love."

Arching her body against his, she placed her mouth on top of his until their mouth met in a soft, wet kiss.

Cupping his hand around her nape, Ronald intensely looked into his loving wife's face, and his heart melted. Never had he ever felt that type of love with any woman he had ever been with.

"Thank you, God," he whispered aloud.

"Yes, Lord, thank you," Allison joined softly. "Thank you for this unexpected love."

*****

Good Judgement

Dear Readers:

Y ou asked for it, and I hope I delivered. You have just finished the sequel to my debut book, *"A Leap of Faith."* This holiday season, I hope you enjoyed reading *"An Unexpected Love for Christmas"* as much as I enjoyed bringing back Allison, Leilani, Floyd, Zora, and Dr. Almah. Not to mention the new characters, Ronald, Ronalda, Deniece, Michael, Judge Gallant, Novak, and baby Alijah!

I do hope that this book opened some eyes for those of us who have been seeking a love of our own but still have unsuccessfully found that person because of our own doing and judgmental ways.

We have all, at some point in our personal life, judged someone not worthy to get to know or start a relationship with, right? Some of us may have even judged our own self as being not good enough for a particular person. This superficial behavior has been displayed by all of us at one point or the other. Instead of getting to know a person and listening to our discernment about a person, we automatically jump to judge.

We are human, and we are visual people, but at some point, we have to get over the visual and base things on accurate information and thy own understanding. As it states in John 7:24, *"Stop judging by the way things look and make a right judgment."*

Judging is a sin, and our God is love. HE is watching how we treat people and how we show love to his children. Because after all, he created each of us in HIS own image. If you can recall in the Bible, Jesus was the one who initiated a conversation with the Samaritan woman in John 4:7-9. He didn't care about what she looked like, her background, her heritage, or anything to that nature. Jesus accepted the woman for who she was, and he offered eternal life to her.

If you are seeking a true love of your own, with the Lord at the head of it, then you need to throw away any checklist or perception you have of the mate you want and strive to live your life in a less judgmental state. Train yourself to interact with others with sincere compassion, forgiveness, grace, mercy, and love. That is how Jesus does.

Quit judging people solely on what they look like and get to know the person. Their heart, their soul, their character, and I can promise you. If you do that, you will find your soulmate and, in the process, you just might be changed.

Always Be A Blessing and as stated in 1 Samuel 25:33: *"May you be blessed for your good judgment…"*

About the Author

A mazon best-selling author Tam Yvonne makes her home on the outskirts of Atlanta, Georgia, with her two teenagers, "the Luv Bugs" and her Shih Tzu fur baby, "Blue." She has garnered much acclaim for her writing style and her debut book, *"A Leap of Faith."* She is also the author of the devotional, *"Be Still~21-Days of Daily Inspirations on Trusting God to Lead You to A Path of Peace."*

She is a lover & follower of Jesus, writer/author, motivational speaker, and educator who spends most of her time reading, writing, cooking, and traveling the world as she often did growing up as an Army brat.

An admitted "people watcher," she feeds her addiction of people watching by creating fictional stories and characters that are both relatable and make sense.

For updates on the goings-on of Tam Yvonne, visit:
www.tamtheauthor.com

 The Author Tam Yvonne

 @TamTheAuthor

Books by Tam Yvonne

A Leap of Faith

Be Still ~ 21-Days of Daily Inspirations on Trusting
God to Lead You to A Path of Peace

An Unexpected Love for Christmas

All books available at Amazon, Barnes & Noble, Books-A-
Million, Wal-Mart, Pen Legacy Publishing &
www.tamtheauthor.com

CPSIA information can be obtained
at www.ICGtesting.com
Printed in the USA
BVHW061603221121
622225BV00008B/334